UP AND DOWN
THE ESCALATOR

a Bill Martin Instant Reader

HOLT, RINEHART AND WINSTON, INC.
New York, Toronto, London, Sydney

UP AND DOWN THE ESCALATOR

by Bill Martin, Jr.

with pictures by Kelly Oechsli

Up and down the escalator,

Up and down the street,

DIRECTORY·

MAIN FLOOR
BASEBALLS
COOKIES
DOLLS

2d FLOOR
TOYS

3d FLOOR
BIKES
BOOKS
COSTUMES
·

Up and down
the elevator,
Shopping is a treat.

In and out of

the candy store,

In and out of the park,

In and out of the
fire hydrant,

Playing after dark.

Over and under

the river bridge,

Over and under the fence,

Over and under the loop-de-loop,

For only fifteen cents.

On and off the ocean liner,

On and off the bus,

On and off the subway train,

Traveling is for us.

All around the   neighborhood,

All around the square,

All around the Christmas tree,

Music everywhere!